Dear Parent:
Your child's love of reading starts here!

Every child learns to read in a different way and at his or her own speed. Some go back and forth between reading levels and read favorite books again and again. Others read through each level in order. You can help your young reader improve and become more confident by encouraging his or her own interests and abilities. From books your child reads with you to the first books he or she reads alone, there are I Can Read Books for every stage of reading:

SHARED READING
Basic language, word repetition, and whimsical illustrations, ideal for sharing with your emergent reader

BEGINNING READING
Short sentences, familiar words, and simple concepts for children eager to read on their own

READING WITH HELP
Engaging stories, longer sentences, and language play for developing readers

READING ALONE
Complex plots, challenging vocabulary, and high-interest topics for the independent reader

I Can Read Books have introduced children to the joy of reading since 1957. Featuring award-winning authors and illustrators and a fabulous cast of beloved characters, I Can Read Books set the standard for beginning readers.

A lifetime of discovery begins with the magical words "I Can Read!"

Visit www.icanread.com for information
on enriching your child's reading experience.

Visit www.zonderkidz.com/icanread for more faith-based
I Can Read! titles from Zonderkidz.

Where you go I will go,
and where you stay I will stay.
—*Ruth 1:16*

ZONDERKIDZ

Ruth and Naomi
Copyright © 2015 by Zondervan
Illustrations © 2015 by David Miles

An **I Can Read Book**

Requests for information should be addressed to:
Zonderkidz, 3900 Sparks Drive SE, Grand Rapids, Michigan 49546

ISBN 978-0-31074650-8

Editor: Mary Hassinger
Art direction and design: Kris Nelson

Printed in China

19 20 /DSC / 21 20 19 18 17 16 15 14 13 12 11 10 9 8 7 6 5 4 3

Adventure BIBLE

Ruth and Naomi

Pictures by David Miles

Naomi grew up in Israel.

She was happy there.

But for a long time, there was no rain.

Nothing could grow.

Naomi had a husband and two sons.

They were hungry and thirsty.

Naomi and her family had to move

far away to Moab.

One day, something bad happened.

Naomi's husband died.

Later, her sons died too.

Naomi was very sad.

Her family was all gone,

and she was far away from Israel.

Naomi decided to go home to Israel.

Her sons' wives wanted to go too.

Their names were Orpah and Ruth.

Orpah and Ruth loved Naomi.

But Naomi shook her head.

She said, "Go back.

Do not come with me.

Stay here with your families."

Orpah and Ruth cried.

They did not want to leave Naomi.

Finally, Orpah said goodbye.

But Ruth said, "I will go with you.

Where you stay, I will stay.

Your people will be my people.

Your God will be my God."

Naomi loved Ruth.

She let Ruth come.

Naomi and Ruth walked to Israel.

It was a long walk.

When they arrived, the people said,

"Naomi is back!"

She was happy to be home.

Ruth and Naomi were very poor.

But Ruth worked hard to find food.

She wanted to take care of Naomi.

Every day, Ruth went out in the fields.

She picked up the grain

that was left behind.

It was hard work.

A man named Boaz owned the field.

Boaz saw Ruth picking up grain.

Boaz asked, "Who is that?"

A worker said,

"She is from far away.

She came here with Naomi

and she works very hard."

Boaz was impressed by Ruth.

He told her, "You can take as much grain as you want from my fields.

I will keep you safe."

Ruth asked,

"Why are you so kind to me?"

Boaz said, "I have heard

of all you have done for Naomi.

You are a good woman."

That evening, Ruth brought home

lots of grain.

Naomi was very happy.

She asked,

"Who helped you with all of this?"

Ruth said, "A man named Boaz."

Naomi smiled.

She said, "Boaz! He is my relative.

He is a good man!

You will be safe in his fields."

Naomi told Ruth,

"Keep working in Boaz's fields."

So Ruth worked in his fields

until the harvest was finished.

Boaz watched Ruth work.

He saw how kind she was to Naomi.

Before long,

Boaz fell in love with Ruth.

One day, Naomi said to Ruth,

"You are still young.

You should get married again.

Then you can have children.

You should marry Boaz."

So Ruth went to Boaz.

He was working in the barn.

Boaz saw her and loved her.

He said, "I want to marry you!"

So Boaz and Ruth got married!

Ruth was very happy.

She had a husband again.

And he was a very kind man.

Naomi was happy too.

She knew that Ruth and Boaz

would take care of her.

She was so thankful,

she jumped in the air!

Later, Ruth and Boaz had a baby boy.

They named him Obed.

Naomi was his grandmother.

What a beautiful family!

Ruth and Naomi thanked God.
They had had a hard life,
but God had blessed them
with a brand-new family!

A long time later,
baby Obed grew up.

He had a son
named Jesse.

And then Jesse had a
son named David.
David became a king.

30

And a long, long time later,

one of David's relatives had a baby.

This baby was Jesus!

So God blessed Ruth.

She became a very-great grandma

to the Savior of the World.

People in Bible Times

May the LORD reward you for what you have done.
May you be richly rewarded by the LORD, the God of Israel.
Ruth 2:12

Ruth

Ruth was a Moabite woman who married a man from Bethlehem. When her husband died, she went to live and help support her mother-in-law, Naomi. Ruth was a kind and loving daughter to Naomi.

Naomi

Naomi was a woman living in Moab. When her husband and sons died, she decided to go home to the town of Bethlehem. She had a daughter-in-law named Ruth, who decided to travel with her back to her hometown.

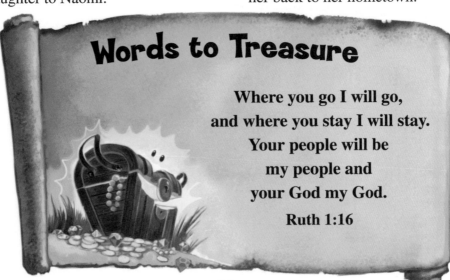

Words to Treasure

**Where you go I will go,
and where you stay I will stay.
Your people will be
my people and
your God my God.**

Ruth 1:16

This book belongs to

_____

Ninja Life Hacks™

This book is dedicated to my children - Mikey, Kobe, and Jojo.
Mistakes and failures help us grow. They are a blessing in disguise.

Perfect ninja loved to do things perfectly.

In fact, when he made a mistake, he would often get upset and sometimes even give up.

For example...

If he was losing during a soccer game, he would stop trying.

If the answers didn't come to him right away while doing homework, he would get frustrated and cry.

And if he messed up while he was
painting, he would scream!

Perfect Ninja had to be perfect under all circumstances. From his perspective there was no time or room for mistakes.

But that all changed during...

...a soccer game!

Perfect Ninja and his teammates had practiced all season for the championship. He took extra time right before the big day to perfect his techniques and strategies.

But it was no match for the Kingpins that year.
They were leading 2-1.

During halftime, Gritty Ninja gave Perfect Ninja a compliment.

"Yeah...but you didn't give up. You kept trying and changed strategies. It takes grit to keep competing. And I think you're doing awesome," said Gritty Ninja.

"It's okay not to be perfect. No one is. Mistakes help us grow," encouraged Gritty Ninja.

For the remainder of the game, Perfect Ninja played his heart out, not caring about making mistakes or failing.

And do you know what?

It worked! The ninjas came back and won it!

After that game, Perfect Ninja adopted a growth mindset. He understood that mistakes were a normal step of the process. And as long as he was learning from them, he would succeed.

Your best weapon against perfectionism is to accept that failure is part of the journey.

As long as you learn and grow from your mistakes, you will succeed.

Download free printables at NinjaLifeHacks.tv

@marynhin   @GrowGrit
#NinjaLifeHacks

Mary Nhin   Grow Grit

Grow Grit

Made in the USA
Columbia, SC
07 January 2021